lunch

This book is for Rochelle

Special thanks to Laura for her patience and
to David and Indigo for their endurance

Henry Holt and Company, Inc.
Publishers since 1866
115 West 18th Street
New York, New York 10011

Henry Holt is a registered trademark of Henry Holt and Company, Inc.

Published in Canada by Fitzhenry & Whiteside Ltd.,
195 Allstate Parkway, Markham, Ontario L3R 4T8.

Library of Congress Cataloging-in-Publication Data
Fleming, Denise.
Lunch/written and illustrated by Denise Fleming.
Summary: A very hungry mouse eats a large lunch
comprised of colorful foods.
[1. Mice—Fiction. 2. Food habits—Fiction. 3. Color—Fiction.]
I. Title. PZ7.F5994Lu 1993 [E]—dc20 92-178

ISBN 0-8050-1638-8 (hardcover)
10 9 8 7 6 5
ISBN 0-8050-4646-1 (paperback)
10 9 8 7 6 5 4

First published in hardcover in 1992 by Henry Holt and Company, Inc.
First paperback edition, 1995

Printed in the United States of America on acid-free paper. ∞

The illustrations were created in handmade paper.

lunch
Denise Fleming

Henry Holt and Company   •   New York

Mouse was *very* hungry.
He was so hungry,

he ate
a crisp
white —

turnip,

tasty

orange —

carrots,

sweet
yellow —

corn,

tender
green —

peas,

tart

blue —

berries,

sour

purple —

grapes,

shiny
red —

apples,

and juicy pink —

watermelon,

crunchy
black seeds
and all.

Then,

he took a nap
until . . .

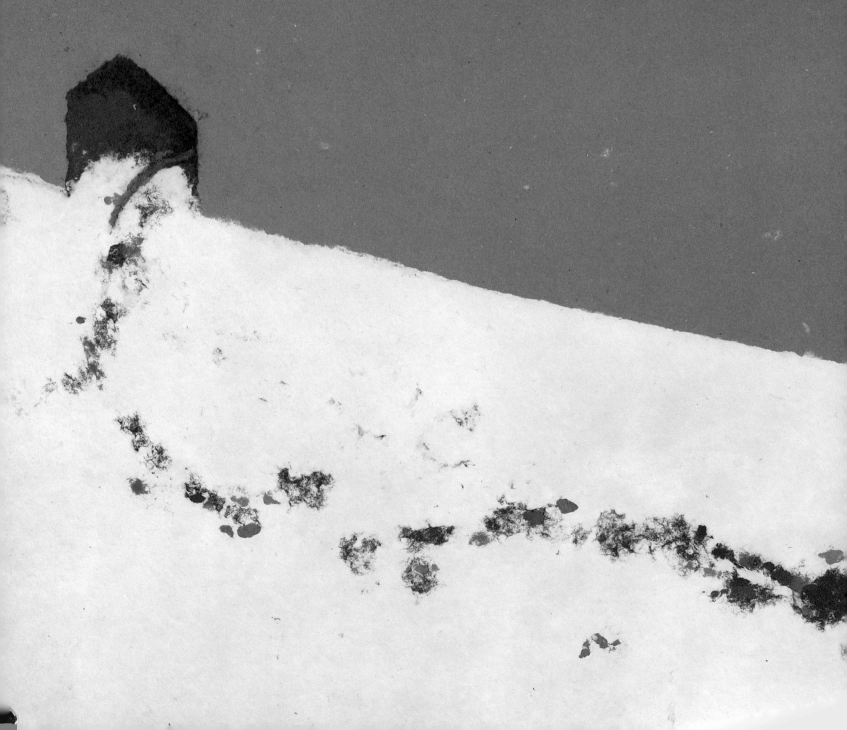

. . . dinnertime!

sniff
sniff

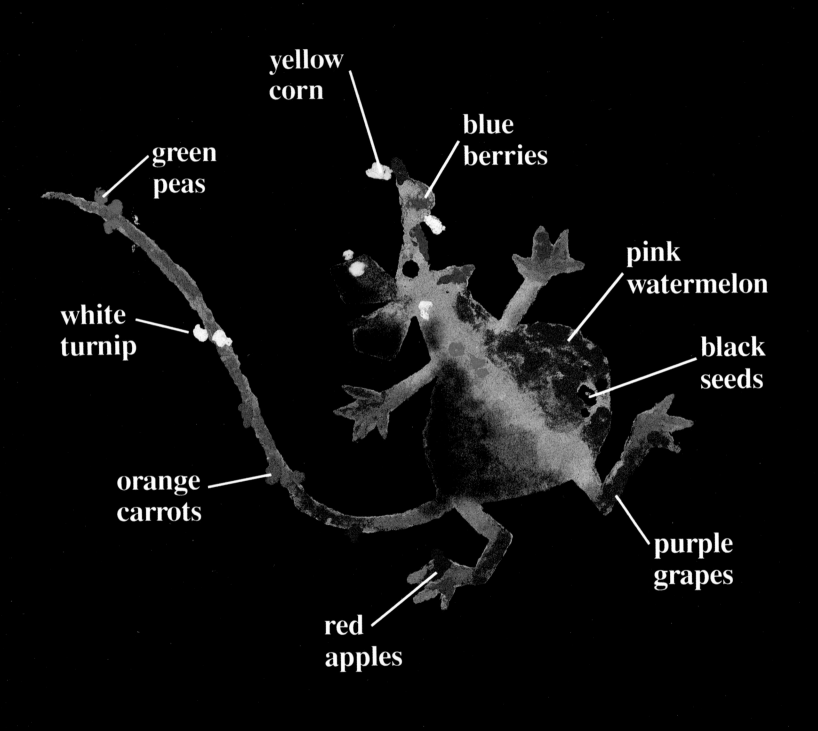

green
peas

yellow
corn

blue
berries

white
turnip

pink
watermelon

black
seeds

orange
carrots

purple
grapes

red
apples